YETTA
THE TRICKSTER

YETTA
THE TRICKSTER

by Andrea Griffing Zimmerman
pictures by Harold Berson

A Clarion Book
The Seabury Press · New York

To my mother and father

The Seabury Press, 815 Second Avenue, New York, New York 10017

Library of Congress Cataloging in Publication Data

Zimmerman, Andrea Griffing.   Yetta, the trickster.
"A Clarion book."
SUMMARY: Yetta loves to play tricks on people until
one day the joke is on her.
[1. Practical jokes—Fiction]
I. Berson, Harold. II. Title.
PZ7. Z618Ye   [Fic]   78-6164   ISBN 0-8164-3218-X

CONTENTS

1

BONK, BONK, BONK!

Yetta bounced into the village on the back of the cart. Today her mother was selling potatoes at the market. Yetta jumped down from the cart. She and her mother waved goodbye.

For a while Yetta looked in shop windows. Then she jumped mud puddles in the street. But before long Yetta wanted to play a joke.

She climbed the apple tree in the village.

A fine lady walked by.
Bonk!
"Stop that!"
Bonk!
"You bad girl!"
Bonk!
The woman ran away.

A boy walked by.

Bonk!

"Hey! Cut that out!"

Bonk!

"I'll get you!" he said.

Bonk! Bonk! Bonk!

The boy ran away.

A dog walked by.
Bonk!
"Woof!"
Bonk!
"Woof, woof!"
Bonk!
The dog ran away.
Yetta bonked everyone who walked by.
Later, in the afternoon, a girl passed.
Bonk!

"Who did that?" the girl said.

"I did!" said Yetta proudly. "It's a joke."

"How funny," said the girl. "I bet you can't do it again."

Yetta laughed.

She threw another apple.

"Missed!" said the girl as she put the apple in a sack. "Try again."

Yetta threw another apple.

"Missed again!"

Yetta tried over and over to bonk her.

Each time the girl put the apple in her sack.

Yetta began to get tired.

The joke wasn't quite as funny now.

"Try again," the girl said.

Yetta threw apples at her until Yetta had picked every apple she could reach.

She was so tired she leaned against a branch.

"Is that all?" said the girl.

"Yes," panted Yetta.

"Too bad," the girl said. "It was a funny joke."

"Yes," sighed Yetta.

"Since you like jokes so much I will tell you a funnier one," said the girl. "I am going to the market to sell these apples you have worked so hard to pick for me!"

With that the girl ran down the path, laughing.

"Hmmm," thought Yetta, "Tomorrow I will pick more apples and sell them myself."

She climbed down the tree.

"I deserve something out of this for all my hard work," said Yetta.

Bonk!

THE WHAT DAY

Yetta was cozy under the quilts in her little attic room.

"Yetta! It is time for school." She wished she did not hear her mother calling.

Then Yetta got an idea. It made her giggle. She jumped out of bed and pulled on her clothes.

She climbed downstairs.

"Good morning," said Mother.

Yetta pretended she did not hear. She looked at her mother and smiled.

"Good morning," Mother said again.

Yetta wrinkled her face. "What?" she said loudly.

"Good morning!" yelled Mother.

"Oh, good morning," said Yetta. She ate her bread and butter.

"Yetta, go collect the eggs," said Mother.

Yetta looked out the window, humming.

"Yetta!" yelled her mother.

She looked at her mother and smiled.

"Oh, I hope your father in heaven is watching," said Mother. She sent Yetta's sister to the hen house instead.

Yetta pinched herself to keep from giggling.

When she left for school, Mother gave her a
letter for the schoolmistress.

It said, "Yetta cannot hear so good today."

Yetta ran to school. She made a sad face
when she gave Miss Petsky her letter. Inside she
was laughing.

"All right," the teacher said.

Yetta wrinkled her face. "What?" she said loudly.

Miss Petsky did not like loud talking. She raised her voice a little and said, "That will be fine."

"What?" yelled Yetta.

"SIT DOWN!"

"Oh," said Yetta, hiding her smile from the teacher.

The children watched with amazement as she took her seat.

At first Yetta was having a wonderful time. She did not have to do any lessons.

But the morning passed very slowly.

She got tired of looking at a book. She did not get to recite with the others.

21

Then Miss Petsky asked a question that no one could answer.

Without thinking, Yetta called out, "I know!" Then she remembered. "Oh, what did you say?"

The class looked at her suspiciously. They whispered to one another.

When school was over, the children gathered around Yetta. "Now I will have some fun," she thought.

"You cannot hear?" asked one.

"What?" yelled Yetta.

"She is like our old deaf cat," said a girl. They laughed.

"She is more like an old toad!" said a boy.

"What?" yelled Yetta. What did he mean she was like a toad? That made her mad.

"Yetta is a toad! Yetta is a toad!" they called.
"She eats flies!" said a boy.
"Her hair is green!" said a girl.
They were all laughing. All except Yetta.
"I have to go home!" she yelled.
She ran all the way.

"Mother, Mother," Yetta said as she hugged her. "My friends did not know I could hear them.

They think I am a toad with green hair who eats flies."

"What?" said her mother.

"My friends did not know I could hear them. They think I am a toad."

"What?" said her mother very loudly.

Yetta started to yell. "My friends did not know I could hear . . ."

She stopped and looked at her mother.

Her mother was laughing.

Yetta started to smile. Her mother had tricked her! She thought for a moment. Her friends had fooled her too! Yetta hugged her mother tightly, and they laughed and laughed.

THE BIG BOO

Yetta's mother was in the kitchen making breakfast one morning.

Yetta crept up behind her. She took very soft steps.

"Boo!" said Yetta.

"Eeeekk!" screamed Yetta's mother as a pancake went flying.

Yetta hugged her mother. "I'm sorry," she said. "I thought you knew I was there!"

Yetta ran outside. She saw her sister digging in the garden. Yetta's footsteps made no sound in the soft dirt.

"Boo!" she said.

"Aaaahhh!" yelled her sister, swinging her hoe around.

Yetta giggled. "I'm sorry, I thought you knew I was there!"

She went to the barn.

Inside she saw Bushka the cow waiting to be milked.

Yetta crept through the hay. "Boo!" she said, popping up suddenly.

Bushka jumped back, then let out a long mournful, "Moo-o-o-o-o."

"I'm sorry, I thought you knew I was here," Yetta giggled, stroking the cow's soft nose.

Yetta went to the hen house. She peeked in and saw the chickens sitting quietly on their nests.

She burst through the door.

"Booo!" she said.

Flying feathers and loud cackling filled the air.

"I'm sorry, I thought you knew I was here."
Yetta smoothed their ruffled feathers.

When there was no one on the farm left to
trick, Yetta went to the village.

"Boo!" she said to the baker.

"Boo!" she said to the grocer.

"Boo!" she said to the dogs on the street.

31

Yetta had a wonderful time. Late in the afternoon, when she was tired, she went home.

The next morning Yetta woke up thinking about how much she had enjoyed herself.

"What's good yesterday is good today," she thought.

Quietly Yetta climbed downstairs.

Her mother was not in the kitchen making breakfast.

"How strange," thought Yetta.

She went outside.

Her sister was not digging in the garden.

Bushka the cow was not in the barn.

The chickens were not in the hen house.

No one was on the farm.

"I hope I have not scared them all away," thought Yetta.

She walked to the village. There was no one on the street.

"How strange," thought Yetta.

She peeked in houses and shops.

The baker was not in the bakery.

The grocer was not in the grocery.

The dogs were not on the street.

Yetta looked everywhere.

No one was anywhere.

"Hello?" called Yetta in a tiny voice. "Where is everyone?"

No one answered. Everything was quiet in the empty village.

Up ahead Yetta saw a big barn.

"Squeeeeeaak," went the door as she slowly opened it.

"BOOOOO!" yelled a huge voice in the dark.

"Eeeeeek!" screamed Yetta, jumping back.

Every single villager was standing in the barn. And they were all laughing.

The baker said, "Oh, we're sorry. We thought you knew we were here."

The people laughed, the chickens clucked, the cows mooed, and the dogs barked.

Even Yetta laughed, because Yetta loved a good trick.

4

THE BEAUTIFUL BUTTER MOLDS

One day Yetta wanted to buy her mother some beautiful butter molds.

Yetta also wanted to play a trick.

She went to milk her cow.

"Good girl, Bushka," she said to her pet.

Yetta hid more than half the milk and then went to her mother.

"Look, Mother," she said.

"My, my," said her mother. "There is not enough milk to sell to the dairy man, but there is enough to make butter with. Times are good, do not worry."

Yetta ran to the dairy with the hidden milk. She sold it and saved the coins.

The next day when Yetta milked her cow she hid more milk.

"Look, Mother," she said.

"My, my," said her mother. "There is not enough milk to make butter with, but there is enough to make yogurt. I wonder if the cow is going dry."

Yetta ran to the dairy laughing. Again she saved the coins.

The next day when Yetta milked her cow she only took a small portion to her mother.

"My, my," said her mother. "There is not enough milk for making yogurt. There is only enough for Catty to lap. Times are bad."

Yetta ran to the dairy. She would soon have enough coins to buy the beautiful butter molds.

The next day Yetta milked her cow.

She showed her mother a tiny bit of milk.

"My, my," said her mother. "There is not enough milk for Catty to lap. There is only enough to curse at! Something must be done."

Yetta hurried to the village. She now had enough coins. She bought the beautiful butter molds.

Yetta was so proud of her trick.

But when she returned home no one was there.

She saw a note:

Dear Yetta,
A woman whose husband is in heaven
must feed her family. If the cow will not
give us food to eat then we are going to
eat the cow. I have gone to the butcher.

"Oh, no," said Yetta. "My lovely Bushka!
Look what my trick has done!"

Yetta ran down the road to the butcher's.

What if it was too late?

"Stop! Stop!" called Yetta.

Her mother was just giving Bushka to the butcher.

Yetta told the whole story as fast as a brook tumbles over stones.

"What a trick!" said her mother. "But what beautiful butter molds."

Bushka blinked sleepily as Yetta hugged her.

They all walked home together.

Yetta's mother carried the butter molds.

Yetta led Bushka. She was thinking of how lucky they were to still have a cow to give milk to make beautiful molded butter.

"I won't play any more tricks . . ." said Yetta, "for a long time."

"That's good," said her mother.

Then Yetta wondered: How long is a long time?

"Maybe I'd better start thinking up tricks," she thought, "so I'll be ready when the long time is over."